For all the kids in my life: my students, my own, and those I have met and will meet along the way. Thank you for reminding me to have a sense of wonder and to see the world with my whole heart.
—S.V.

For my son, Luca, who sees everything with wonder
—J.P.

The illustrations in this book were made digitally.

Cataloging-in-Publication Data has been applied for and may be obtained from the Library of Congress.

ISBN 978-1-4197-6163-8

Text © 2023 Susan Verde
Illustrations © 2023 Juliana Perdomo
Book design by Heather Kelly

Printed and bound in China
10 9 8 7 6 5 4 3 2 1

Abrams Books for Young Readers are available at special discounts when purchased in quantity for premiums and promotions as well as fundraising or educational use. Special editions can also be created to specification. For details, contact specialsales@abramsbooks.com or the address below.

ABRAMS The Art of Books
195 Broadway, New York, NY 10007
abramsbooks.com

an You SEE It?

by

SUSAN VERDE

illustrated by

JULIANA PERDOMO

Abrams Books for Young Readers

New York

When I am busy—
moving through my day,
watching where I go—

looking shows me
what is right in front of my eyes.

But when I slow down—
find stillness, and notice
with patience and curiosity—

I can see.

Seeing shows me more.

I can look at a tree . . .

Can you see it?

AUTHOR'S NOTE

The world is a sensory experience. We look, hear, taste, touch, and smell what is all around us. And when one of our senses isn't accessible, we turn to others to help us navigate our lives. But sometimes we move so quickly through our days that we forget to stop and pay attention. What would happen if we were to slow down and go a little deeper with our senses? Instead of just *looking* at all that is around us, what if we tried *seeing*? Have you ever thought about the difference? Seeing asks that we take time to notice not only the details, but also the information and the feelings we get from what is in front of us. When we see, we find we can be curious, make discoveries, and be more connected to our lives.

Can You See It? is all about taking a longer look and seeing what is miraculous in this big universe. It's my hope that this book will lead to an exploration of and conversation about what it means to really *see* one another, nature, the world—not just with our eyes, but with our whole hearts. Can you see love? Friendship? The wonder of nature? What does that look like to you? You may be surprised by what you notice and what it makes you feel inside.

Try the following exercise to practice seeing. You can be inside or outside, seated or standing, alone or with a group, wherever you may be. Here is a seated version.

Take a comfortable seat and begin with your eyes closed. Breathing in and out through your nose, start to notice your own breath without trying to change or force it. Just give yourself a moment to be fully present. When you are ready, open your eyes and look straight ahead at what is in front of you. It may not be anything surprising at first, but start to notice all the details. What is its shape, color, size? Are there shadows? Is it moving or still? What is happening in the spaces in between or around it? What is that object showing you about itself? Maybe a flower is shaped a certain way to attract a butterfly. Maybe the color of a leaf is an early sign of fall. Finally, bring your attention to how it makes you feel inside. Is there joy or a sense of beauty? Is there sadness or confusion? There is no wrong answer, only what you see. Now close your eyes once more. Holding on to all that you saw and all that you wondered and felt, take a deep breath in and out through your nose, then gently open your eyes once again.

The practice of mindfulness is one way to cultivate a deeper relationship with your world by using your senses to be in the present moment. When we pause, breathe, and notice, we can be curious and see more.

It can be fun to write your thoughts and feelings down, or to talk about them during or after this exercise. You can even create a piece of art or tell a story based on what you discover when you take the time to *see*.

But seeing is the feeling in our bellies
when we realize the world is full of miracles.

This glorious universe has so much to share.

Glowing from the inside out.
Your creativity,
your compassion,
your joy.
All that makes you YOU.

What can *you* see?

We can look.

A hug just when it's needed.

A warm meal made to share.

What can *you* see?

but I can see love.

Time together.

A smile that says,
"I am happy you are here."

Making space for everyone.

Attention to little things
that make a big
difference.

What can *you* see?

I can look at my family . . .

Floating,
flying, arching, sparkling.
An invitation to stay in or go out,
rest or play.

What can *you* see?

I can look at a friend . . .

but I can see beauty.

Old mixed with new,
life in unexpected places,

moments of calm in the hustle and bustle.
A story of community.

What can *you* see?

I can look at the sky...

but I can see magic.

Signs of change and letting go,
flowering and feeding,
shading and sheltering.
A place to call home.

What can *you* see?

I can look at a city block . . .

but I can see life.

I can look at myself . . .

and I can see my inner light shine.
Can you see yours?